Brooklyn

...n massaged her arm to relieve th...
that radiated [illegible] kind
tunnel syn[illegible] look
numb. But [illegible]
ne she was forced to work through
ain. Taking a break from her manu...
t the writer logged onto Facebook
red notification light lit up in the [illegible] received
ber of the [illegible] She didn't
tiple friend requests a day. She'd simp...
ly think much of them.
nd a few minutes each night approv...
requests. With the release of
rd bestselling book and her regular
rance on CNN she was becoming
easingly popular. But when one of
cent followers listed her as a fa...
ember it caused her alarm. "Alisa D...
as listed you as a family member. D...
lick the link to approve."
The Facebook message flashed a...
her screen. Brooklyn wrinkled her
She stared at the screen and the
[illegible] to familiarize herself with
[illegible] He scrolled throu...

Brooklyn

a novel by

KRYSTAL GRANT

ALSO BY KRYSTAL GRANT

Under the Palmetto Tree: A Novella

The Miseducation of Ms. G

Brooklyn

Krystal Grant

F I R S T   E D I T I O N

ISBN: 978-1-942545-03-3
Library of Congress Control Number: to come

ALL RIGHTS RESERVED
©2015 Krystal Grant

No part of this publication may be translated, reproduced or transmitted in any form without prior permission in writing from the publisher. Publisher and editor are not liable for any typographical errors, content mistakes, inaccuracies, or omissions related to the information in this book.

Cover Photo © Ginasanders | Dreamstime.com
Ladies Shoes And Mortarboard

Blogalicious is a trademark of Stacey Ferguson, used with permission.

Published by Kenely Books, An Imprint of Wyatt-MacKenzie
kenely@wyattmackenzie.com

For Rodney,
Madison, Collin, and Chase,
James and Okla Kenely,
Cheryl, Terri, Jamilia, and Kayela

Chapter 1

BROOKLYN MASSAGED HER ARM to relieve the ache that radiated through her wrist. Carpal tunnel syndrome left her hand nearly numb. But with an impending book deadline she was forced to work through the pain. Taking a break from her manuscript the writer logged onto Facebook. The red notification light lit up in the corner of the webpage. Brooklyn received multiple friend requests a day. She didn't really think much of them. She'd simply spend a few minutes each night approving the requests. With the release of her third bestselling book and her regular appearance on CNN she was becoming increasingly popular. But when one of her recent followers listed her as a family member it caused her alarm. *"Alisa Daniels has listed you as a family member. Please click the link to approve."*

The Facebook message flashed across her screen. Brooklyn wrinkled her brow. She stared at the screen

and thought- trying to familiarize herself with the name. She quickly scrolled through the names on her friend list. She clicked on Alisa Daniels name and analyzed the photo. Brooklyn didn't recognize the woman. They had no mutual friends and no similar interests. She took note that the woman lived in Atlanta. She thought that since they resided in the same city their paths may have crossed on occasion. Brooklyn decided to leave Alisa a message:
"Hi there! I see you added me as a family member. Please remind me how we know each other."

After responding to a few emails Brooklyn printed her flight itinerary and zipped her suitcase. The four hour flight to Las Vegas would provide her with uninterrupted time to edit her fourth novel. The impending deadline was fast approaching. And while she assured her editor that the book would be completed in time, she was unsure how it would get done.

Hartsfield-Jackson International Airport was a hub of activity. Travelers rushed through the terminals with their luggage trailing behind them. Brooklyn sat at Gate B watching a slew of passersby. A mother sat at the gate breastfeeding her newborn. A powder blue blanket was slung over her shoulder concealing the suckling child. Brooklyn gazed in wonder at the woman. She closed her eyes and imagine what it felt like to nurse an infant. Brooklyn's mind took her back to the year prior. She laid in her hospital bed curled into a ball. Her eyes were wet with tears. The emergency room doctor had delivered the terrible news earlier that day but she remained in shock. *"You've had a miscarriage. The fetus was unable to survive the shock of the car accident. I'm so sorry."* After months of couple's therapy Brooklyn and the baby's father, Brian, had finally reconnected. She reconciled her feelings of anger towards him for speeding through the red light- causing the accident.

Brooklyn's gaze refocused on the powder blue blanket. She watched the woman gather her things and hand her boarding pass to the flight attendant at the gate. It was time to board the plane.

Settling into her seat, Brooklyn pulled out her phone and composed a text: *"About to take off for Vegas. Love you."* Then turned her phone off. The baby, wrapped in the powder blue blanket, let out a loud wail. His mother repositioned him in her arms and rocked him slowly. Brooklyn watched the mother pull a pacifier from her bag and place it in the baby's mouth. The woman's brown Burberry bag was pressed against the seat in front of her. A matching wallet slid from the purse onto the airplane floor. As the woman quickly snatched the chocolate wallet from the floor and toss it back in her bag the flight attendants began to deliver safety instructions to the passengers. Brooklyn fastened her seatbelt and rested her head on the back of her chair as the attendants talked. She thought to check her phone again before take off for any messages from Brian. But Brooklyn knew that he would have limited wi-fi access for the next few weeks so communication with him would be scant. He had left for Ocho Rios, Jamaica a few days prior to assist in the rebuilding of Trelawny Independent Day School. The school was destroyed by fire a month before. As principal of the Atlanta Leadership Academy for Boys, Brian had developed a successful exchange program with the principal of Trelawny Independent Day school. So, it was fitting that he and other school leaders join in the rebuilding efforts. He would be gone for two weeks.

Brooklyn felt a jolt as the wheels lifted off the tarmac. Her stomach turned with the plane's increasing elevation. She hated plane rides. But with her monthly speaking engagements, conferences and book signings, air travel was a necessary part of her job. She watched the power blue blanket shuffle as the baby stirred. The mother whispered into the baby's ear and secured him in her arms.

Opening her MacBook, Brooklyn stared at her manuscript. She had two chapters that needed to be edited and sent back to her publisher in less than a week. She hoped to finished at least one chapter before the plane landed, but thought it would be difficult since she had become captivated by the baby in the powder blue blanket.

The flight attendant offered Brooklyn a soft drink and continued rolling her cart down the aisle servicing other travelers. Brooklyn held her cup to her lips and felt the fizz from the Coca Cola tickle her nose. The woman holding the baby drank from a bottle of Aquafina water. Here baby had fallen asleep and rested peacefully on the woman's lap. Brooklyn wondered about the child's father. There was a large diamond wedding band on the woman's ring finger. Her manicure was perfectly done and her hair was neat. She has an air of royalty about her. A tone of arrogance that was quite off-putting to Brooklyn. The woman did not seem to be very approachable and didn't acknowledge anyone around her. She did not want to be bothered.

Brooklyn turned her attention to the squeaky cart that moved down the aisle and tossed her cup into the trash as the attendant passed. She typed furiously on her laptop, updating character descriptions and minor details that her editor disliked. She was determined to get this book finished one way or another. The characters had long left her memory since completing the first draft of the book and she was ready to begin work on another idea that had lived inside her head for months. Brooklyn's ears began to pop. She searched for a piece of gum in her purse to relieve the tightness in her ears. The sinus medicine she took that morning was wearing off and she felt the beginnings of another headache. She eyed her watch. It was time to take another dose of the antibiotic her doctor had prescribed. Her double ear infection couldn't have come at a worse time. But as the opening keynote, there was no way she could miss the Blogalicious conference. Brooklyn motioned for the flight attendant and requested a cup of water. The medicine soon gave her some relief which allowed her to finish editing the manuscript.

Brooklyn lifted the window shade and peered out onto the Grand Canyon. It was a massive, gaping whole in the earth. The sun shone brutally on the brown clay. Brooklyn squinted to get a closer look at the national treasure. She thought about Brian. He left for Jamaica the day before and she had already begun to miss him. She was anxious to hear about his flight, the condition of the school, and the mood of the students and staff. Brooklyn imagined the rebuilding efforts to be a daunting task, but she was proud that Brian decided to go with such zeal. He organized the trip quickly and wasted no time collecting money and supplies from their community to send overseas. Brooklyn admired his love for education. She thought him to be a passionate leader and she did her best to encourage his efforts.

The baby in the blue blanket let out another wail. Brooklyn watched as the mother pulled her breast from her designer shirt and latch the baby onto her nipple. The mother quickly covered herself with the blanket. Brooklyn opened a new blank document on her computer and began to type:

Eugenia and Willie

Eugenia's fist met Willie's face with such force it made his teeth rattle. Willie fell to the floor in a slump and did not move. Eugenia was satisfied. She hope her husband was dead. Eugenia gathered a pile of spit in her mouth, spat on him, them slowly sauntered into the kitchen and stirred the pot of collards that were cooking on the stove. It was a hot August day and Eugenia had no time for Willie's foolishness. He was drunk.

Sweat trickled down Eugenia's face as the heat of the collards rose in the air. She licked her lips and thought of various ways she could dispose of Willie's cold, dead, drunk body. Eugenia lowered the flame on her gas stove and placed the lid on her cast iron pot.

Her unfinished game of solitaire waited at the kitchen table. Eugenia gingerly placed her heavy frame in a wooden chair and kicked her pink house shoes onto the floor. A fly buzzed around her ear and landed on the rim of a tea cup which sat on the table. She pulled an ace of spades from the deck of cards and placed it down. Eugenia watched the fly hover over her tea cup. She eyed the pink and green pattern that danced around the cup. Eugenia grinned as she thought of receiving the gift nearly 43 years before, on her wedding day. It was precious. Very delicate, expensive and beautiful.

A stark contrast from her marriage which was defective, useless, and ugly.

Now that her novel was completely edited and ready to be sent to her publisher Brooklyn felt it was safe to begin her next project. This book, based on the lives of her parents, is one that she has wanted to write for years. But knew that she needed to mourn the loss of her parents adequately before beginning such a book. Brooklyn's parents, met as students at Morris College in Sumter, South Carolina. Her mother, Rhonda, was from Greeleyville, South Carolina, a very small town with only a few hundred residents. Her father, Remy, was from Myrtle Beach, a large tourist city positioned near the Atlantic Ocean. Remy was a master musician. His instrument of choice was the trumpet but he was an expert on all brass and woodwinds. Remy taught band at Scott's Branch High School in Summerton, South Carolina for nearly a decade. But his frequent use of alcohol began to take precedence over his teaching career. Brooklyn's father was a drunk. He would come home from a night of heavy drinking, wake his wife from her sleep and attempt to beat her. But Rhonda was no fool. A heavy set woman with high cheekbones and a strong fist, Rhonda never allowed Remy to get the best of her. She slept with a box cutter in her slippers that lay beside her bed. And just in case the box cutter wasn't enough, she kept a butcher's knife under her mattress. When Remy would pull her from the bed in a drunken rage and squeeze at her throat, Rhonda balled her heavy fist and punched him in his ear. Remy stumbled and released his grip. He'd then charge at her, knocking her to the floor. She'd steady herself on her feet and move toward her slippers. Just as she pulled the box cutter from her shoes Remy would grab the back of her head and yank her scarf from her head. Oftentimes, this would cause Rhonda's hair rollers to fall from her head. Rhonda became infuriated at this because of the effort it took her to press and curl her hair. Rhonda would take her box cutter and swing it at Remy, intentionally missing his chest. He then fell backwards onto the floor of their bedroom and lay there in a cold slump until the next afternoon. This was their dance night after night.

Rhonda endured this treatment for years. No one in the community of Summerton, South Carolina was wise about her troubles. Despite her grief, Rhonda arose each morning, made her daughters a breakfast of cheese grits, eggs, bacon and toast, sent the children off to school, then traveled down Highway 15 towards Sumter. Rhonda worked as a nurse at Toumey Regional Hospital. She spent her days in the intensive care unit monitoring life support systems, changing oxygen tanks and consoling grief stricken families. On one particular day, exhausted from an unusually long night of fighting with her husband,

Rhonda arrived at work to learn that her patient, Ola Kendall, had died. The family was on their way to the hospital and Rhonda would be the one to deliver the news. Five girls and their father stood in the hallway of the intensive care unit. It was a quiet morning. The hospital had not begun its usual hustle and bustle of activity. The father, Jimmy, supported his weight with a walking stick- a much needed tool to assist him after hip replacement surgery. The sisters all stood in a similar fashion, arms folded, one leg in front of the other, slowly shuffling their weight from one leg to the other. Rhonda rounded the corner. "*Your mother stopped breathing at 7:50 this morning. We attempted CPR but were unable to revive her. I'm so sorry for your loss.*" Rhonda watched as the girls simultaneously lowered their eyes to the floor. *"We will give you some time with Ola if you'd like. You can follow me."*

The nurse lead the family to a corner room where Ola lay. A gray blanket was pulled taut to her chest. Her fingers had begun to turn blue due to lack of oxygen. The girls circled around the bed while their father took a seat in the corner and rested his head on his cane. Rhonda backed out of the room to allow privacy. She prayed that God would grant Ola's family peace and comfort. She thanked Him for Ola's life and asked that her spirit be taken into Heaven to live for eternity. When Rhonda's prayer was finished she heard singing coming from Ola's room.

I am free.

Thank the Lord I'm free.

No longer bound.

No more chains holding me.

My soul is resting.

And it's a blessing.

Praise the Lord,

Hallelujah! I'm free.

Ola's oldest daughter sang out to God to relieve her sorrow. It was a beautiful moment. One that Rhonda felt honored to be privy to. Rhonda pulled a wad of tissue from her pocket and wiped her eyes.

She arrived home later than usual that evening. The day had proven to be difficult due to the passing of her patient and the stack of paperwork she was required to complete. Just as the sun surrendered to the night sky Rhonda dragged herself through her front door. The television blasted an episode of Sanford and Son. The smell of vodka loomed in the air. An overturned bottle of alcohol lay on the coffee table. Remy had been drinking. Rhonda moved through the living room slowly, in search of her intoxicated husband. She dared not wake him from his drunken slumber. There was no sign of him in the living room. But Rhonda heard the water running in the shower, so she made her way down the hall towards the bathroom. Just as she rounded the corner

Rhonda found her husband standing in the hallway peering into a half-closed bathroom door with his manhood exposed, pleasuring himself. Remy's hand moved back and forth with such force that if he didn't stop soon, he would surely break the thing in pieces. Rhonda stood in horror thinking about her 15 year old daughter, Brooklyn. Remy could not have known what he was doing. Rhonda didn't want to believe that he would ever hurt either of their girls. But she wasn't taking any chances. She picked up a glass vase that sat on a stand in her hallway and smashed it against Remy's head. He fell. It was at that moment Rhonda decided her husband had to go- either he'd leave voluntarily or she would kill him.

The Las Vegas cab driver smelled of cigarette smoke and burning rubber. Brooklyn felt nauseated in the back seat as the driver sped down the freeway. She held on tightly to the car door as the cabbie rounded each curb. His dingy white tank top and scruffy blond beard did nothing to enhance his features. Brooklyn could see the dirt under his fingernails from the back seat. She was afraid. This was her first time in Las Vegas and she was forced to trust this stranger with her life. Brooklyn looked out her window at the sprawling buildings that lined each street. She prayed that God would keep her from all hurt, harm and danger. In the middle of her prayer

Brooklyn's Twitter notification sounded from her phone. She read through her numerous mentions:

> "Excited to finally meet @WritersLife at @BeBlogalicious in Vegas."
>
> "@WritersLife Where are you girl? Can't wait to see you!"
>
> "Just passed @WritersLife in airport on my way to @BeBlogalicious"

Brooklyn favorited each tweet she was mentioned in and sent a tweet of her own:

"Just landed. On my way to @RedRock for @BeBlogalicious. Can't wait."

Instantly, Brooklyn's tweet was favorited nine times and retweeted a total of seventeen times. Her twitter account, @WritersLife, had over 11,000 followers. She used her account to engage her audience and keep fans abreast of her upcoming projects. Each day, Brooklyn would tweet out pertinent advice for writers related to the publishing industry, book marketing and the writing process. Her social media endeavors were the driving force behind the success of her books. Her blog, Facebook, Twitter, and Instagram accounts were effective ways to connect with her readers.

Brooklyn paid the cabbie and jumped out of the vehicle, inhaling the fresh Las Vegas air. The Red Rock Casino Resort and Spa was a sprawling structure with over 100,000 square feet of event space. Brooklyn was greeted at the lobby entrance by massive red doors and a handsome doorman who smiled and tipped his hat to her. She blushed at the attention and made her way to the check-in desk. *"Brooklyn! Brooklyn is that you?"* She turned in the direction of the voice. Selena Frasier, the conference organizer, moved towards her wearing an orange maxi dress that kissed her ankles. Her face was bare with the exception of false eyelashes and lip gloss. There were beads of sweat gathered on her forehead. She looked tired. Selena threw her arms around Brooklyn and squeezed her waist. Brooklyn returned the hug, happy to see her friend. The two women took a selfie in the middle of the hotel lobby, both pausing their conversation to upload the picture to Instagram.

Selena spoke quickly, trying to conceal her Southern drawl. She was a Louisiana native who had moved to Washington DC shortly after graduating law school. She and her husband, Jon Frasier, ran a sports agency in DC and represented athletes in the WNBA, NBA and MLB. Selena asked Brooklyn if she was ready for her presentation. Brooklyn assured her friend that she was prepared and excited to deliver the opening keynote address at the Blogalicious Conference. Selena was disappointed to hear that Brooklyn would not attend the meet-and-greet later that night, but understood how tiring travel could be. She encouraged Brooklyn to get some rest. The pair said their goodbyes as Selena rushed off to prepare for the conference.

Brooklyn stood at the door of her hotel room. Clearly there had been a mistake. The lavish penthouse suite was draped in white décor. The plush sofas sat on top of a white shag carpet. A flat screen TV was positioned atop a marble fireplace. Brooklyn moved slowly through the kitchen, running her fingers over the countertops, also decorated in white marble. Stainless steel appliances lined the walls. Cream colored curtains outlined the floor-to-ceiling windows which gave a fantastic view of the desert landscape. Brooklyn could see mountains in the distance. She watched as an airplane flew across the sky. From the corner of her eye she spotted a bouquet of lilies. She turned towards the glass kitchen table and read the card. "*Welcome to Las Vegas. Enjoy your stay! Love, Blogalicious.*" Brooklyn could not believe that the conference organizers had gifted her with such a room. She was humbled.

Brooklyn peered over into the hot tub that sat in the corner of the bedroom. She wrinkled her nose and wondered the kind of raucous endeavors that had taken place in it. Her queen-sized bed was covered in white linen with a plethora of white throw pillows. She pulled the curtains, allowing the Nevada sun to enter the room. Brooklyn continued her tour of the suite. She grew more and more surprised by each room she entered. Brooklyn sat on the plush bed and composed a text to Selena. *"This room is unbelievable! Thank you! You are so thoughtful."* She didn't expect a response because she knew Selena would be busy readying the event space for the next day's conference so she tossed her phone aside and ordered room service. While waiting for her dinner to arrive Brooklyn unpacked her luggage and took a shower. Just as she dressed herself in a pair of Betsy Johnson pajamas, gifted by Brian, the doorbell rang. *"A doorbell in a hotel?"* Brooklyn said in amusement as she walked to the door to receive her room service order.

After dinner Brooklyn settled into her sumptuous bed, logged onto her blog and began to write:

Because I'm Happy?

I know that happiness isn't tied to material things, or a perfect life. There have been hundreds of books written on the subject of happiness. There are people who make lots of money hosting workshops, panel discussions and talk shows on happiness. And Pharrell William's hit record "Happy" can't find it's way OFF the radio. Heck, we even have a "World Happiness Day". With such emphasis on happiness, why is it that 40 million adults (18% of the American population) suffer from anxiety disorders? Moreover, why is it that women are diagnosed with depression at double the rate than men? What is it that we're searching for that is outside of our grasps? Why can't we all just be happy? It's an easy question. But quite difficult to answer.

Not long after she published the post and shared it on her social media channels there were twelve pending comments. Brooklyn responded to each one, thanking her readers for their thoughts.

That next morning Brooklyn was met with an overwhelming amount of congratulations on her keynote address. All of her blogger friends and fellow entrepreneurs told her how enlightening her talk had been. Brooklyn sat at a reserved table in the front of the ballroom positioned between Langston Harper and Tieffa Taylor. Langonston was the creator of *Black Marriage Works* - an online publication that caters to and promotes African American marriages. Tieffa was the owner of *The Art of Instruction* - a Las Vegas tutorial service for students in grades K-12 - and creator of the nationally known blog, *Miseducation.com.* The table was adorned in a gray cloth with matching chair covers. The centerpieces were miniature candelabras with beads of pearls strung through them.

Brooklyn typed furiously on her MacBook, updating her Facebook page with pictures from the conference. Hundreds of her 20,000 Facebook followers liked the pictures immediately. She twisted her wrist in a circular fashion to relieve the pain of carpal tunnel syndrome as she listened to the next speaker, CEO of Black Enterprise magazine, give entrepreneurial tips to the crowd. She tweeted several notable tips from the speech- all of which were retweeted many times.

At a neighboring table Damon Caine snapped a photo of Brooklyn. She quickly turned towards the flash of the camera. She stared at Damon with little emotion, then turned back to the speaker. Damon Caine was an Atlanta writer who had published six books of poetry on topics ranging from fatherhood to education. He and Brooklyn had been friendly throughout the years, seeing one another at various blogger events held throughout the country. Last winter, at a book release party that Brooklyn hosted for a newly published friend, Damon, who was in attendance, received an emergency call from his wife. Their daughter has suffered an asthma attack and was being rushed to the emergency room. Damon asked Brooklyn to drive him to the hospital, as he had taken the subway to the venue. Brooklyn sympathized with him but as the event host, wasn't able to leave. She offered to call him a cab. Throughout the evening Damon exchanged text messages with Brooklyn, updating her on his daughter's improving health. A few weeks later when the two saw one another again Brooklyn made her way through a crowded room towards him. When Damon spotted Brooklyn he scowled and walked in the opposite direction. Since that time, Damon had unfriended her on all social media accounts. Brooklyn was sad and confused. She felt erased. She had no idea what she had done wrong...if anything. Damon didn't give her an opportunity to find out because her text messages to him had gone unanswered.

The CEO of Black Enterprise concluded his talk and garnered a rousing ovation. He stepped off the side of the stage and posed for a few official photos with Selena before taking his seat. Brooklyn had about ten minutes before her conference sponsored book signing. She quickly closed her laptop and headed towards the doors of the ballroom. As she neared the exit, Selena stood at the microphone and announced the book signing to the group of four hundred attendees. They all cheered. Brooklyn turned and waved to the crowd then headed to her booth.

Later that evening after signing nearly one hundred copies of her book, Brooklyn lounged on the sofa in her suite with a heating pad wrapped around her wrist. Book signings had become increasingly difficult since the nerves in her hand and arm were inflamed by carpal tunnel. She made it to her room just in time to receive a Facetime call on her iPad from Brian. He was doing well. In the few days that he and his companions had been in Ocho Rios they managed to lay the foundation for a new school and erect the framework. Brooklyn didn't have much opportunity to tell Brian about the conference. He spent most of their conversation talking about his work. He was dedicated to rebuilding Trelawny Independent Day

School. In the middle of Brian's rant, Brooklyn drifted off to sleep with an episode of Criminal Minds playing on her flat screen TV.

Awakening from her nap, Brooklyn wiped the line of saliva that formed on the side of her face and opened her MacBook. Fighting against the pain in her wrist she wrote:

Eugenia and Willie

Eugenia poured three cups of sugar in her Kool-Aid mix and stirred. She listened as the water rushed from the showerhead in the bathroom. Willie had finally awakened from his drunken slumber and managed to pull himself from the floor and into the bathroom. Eugenia heard a heavy knock at the door. She lifted the spoon to her lips and tasted the purple liquid. She wiped her mouth then extracted another heap of sugar from its container and dumped it into the Kool-Aid before moving towards the front door.

Laura stood on the porch trembling. She wore a plaid dress with discolored stockings and a gray trench coat. Her attire was too much for the warm spring day. Laura's large afro was a halo around her small head. She shifted her eyes from left to right as she spoke. "Hey, hey, hey, Ms. 'Genia. Can I borrow some bread?" Eugenia looked at Laura with pity. She invited her in, then asked where she was going wearing that trench coat. Laura told her she was on her way to her sister's house. Eugenia cut Laura a large slice of ham that was cooling on the countertop. She placed the ham between two slices of wheat bread, poured a glass of grape Kool-Aid and placed the meal on the table. Laura sat down and stuffed the sandwich into her mouth. Eugenia stared at Laura with pity. When Laura and her twin sister were teenagers, they would spend their summers swimming in Cooter Creek. One June afternoon, when it was remarkably hot, the girls gathered their things and headed to the water. Shortly after jumping in, Laura looked around for her sister. She called out, Paula! Paula! Paula! There was no answer. Laura thought it to be a game so she wasn't alarmed. For thirty minutes she splashed in the creek enjoying the cool of the water. She imagined her sister to be hiding behind a palmetto tree in the distance. Paula's body wasn't found until the next afternoon when the Sherriff's office dragged the lake. She had drowned. Since that time, something had been extremely off about Laura, and understandably so. She began wearing layers and layers of clothing, even in the most scorching weather. She would keep her hands in her pocket, as if concealing something. Laura began to walk at maximum speeds and talk to herself repeatedly. If you listened closely, you could hear the whispers of her sister's name in between other mumbled words. She never went swimming again.

Laura chugged the glass of Kool-Aid and wiped her mouth with the sleeve of her trench coat. She scratched the side of her head and stood to leave. Eugenia offered Laura more to eat, but she refused. She thanked Eugenia for her hospitality and left the house in search of her sister.

Brooklyn's Facebook notification sounded. She clicked on the screen to open the webpage and saw a message waiting. Alisa Daniels sent her a reply. Brooklyn's eyes scanned the screen. " *I listed you as a relative because, well, since we're sleeping with the same man I guess that makes us family*."

"*There must be some mistake*." was the only response that Brooklyn could muster. But she knew it to be true. This was not the first message of its kind that Brooklyn had received from an unfamiliar woman. She had contended with Brian's exploits in the past. Another message popped up on her screen. She took a deep breath before reading it, already feeling exhausted by the situation. "*Brian and I have been seeing each other for a few months now. And I'm pregnant. I just thought you should know.*" Brooklyn rolled her eyes at the screen and let her head fall backward on the couch. "*Damn*" she said. Then she typed, "*Thank you for letting me know. Please don't contact me again*." Brooklyn then blocked the woman from her Facebook page and closed her laptop.

That next morning, Brooklyn sat in on an all star blogger panel. She listen intently as Lisa Garcia, owner of SpanglishSisters.com, discussed the benefits of brand ambassadorship. There were a myriad of questions being asked by attendees and the panel masterfully answered them all. Brooklyn's belly began to rumble and she tried to conceal the sound by holding in her stomach tightly. She had not eaten breakfast. She spent most of the previous night researching various apartment locations around Atlanta. After receiving the message from Alisa Daniels, she decided to move into her own space, away from Brian. She overslept by half an hour so she didn't have time to consume any food before attending the first workshop of the morning. Brooklyn quietly stepped out of the panel discussion and headed to the first floor of the hotel to find some breakfast. As she stepped off of the elevator she became dizzy from the smell of cigarette smoke. The fumes from the hotel casino had made their way through the space. Feeling nauseated, she entered a coffee shop and ordered a cup of yogurt, banana and croissant. She sat at a corner table and ate her breakfast in hopes that the stomach pangs would disappear. As she tossed her garbage in a nearby trash bin Craig Kingston walked into the coffee shop. Craig was wearing Levi jeans and a black t shirt, displaying the name of his blog. "*BlackTechTalk.com*" was etched across his chest. Craig and his brother, Corey, were tech vloggers who filmed a weekly web series. Their vlogs educated readers on the latest must-have gadgets. Craig smiled when he saw Brooklyn sitting in the corner. He hugged her warmly and sat at the table. They spent the next hour updating one another on their lives over the past year. The pair agreed to film a vlog later that day which would appear on Craig's YouTube channel.

On her way back into the conference she received a call from her editor. He had approved the changes she made to her manuscript and was excited about the marketing package he was preparing for the book release. Brooklyn was surprised at the speed at which her editor worked, but felt confident that he would be thorough.

That afternoon Brooklyn had an opportunity to visit the sponsor hall and talk with representatives from various companies. The area was crowded because this conference was the only chance many bloggers had to access such sponsors. Glass doors separated the sponsor hall from an outside patio. A sign sat on a tripod beside the doors. "*Bloggers At Play*" was written in bold letters. Through the glass, Brooklyn could see many of her blogger friends playing double dutch, hop scotch, hula hoop and various other childhood games. She smiled and took several pictures of the group then uploaded them to Instagram. With half an hour until her next workshop, Brooklyn went back to her hotel suite and reclined on the sofa. Just as she closed her eyes her Twitter alert sounded on her phone. @BlackMenCook asked, "*Where are you? @WritersLife*". She gave a crooked smile then responded to her mention with haste. Aaron Gentry was a food blogger and ran the popular website www.BlackMenCook.com . He lived in Chicago and worked as a personal chef to the Mayor of the city. A few minutes after responding to the Twitter mention, Brooklyn's doorbell rang. She rushed to the door and without hesitation jumped into Aaron's arms. They embraced one another at length.

"Look what I brought you!" Aaron showed Brooklyn a family sized bag of barbecue potato chips. She squealed with glee and they both laughed. *"This is why I can't ever get a six pack,"* Brooklyn joked as she opened the bag and pulled out a handful of chips.

The friends sat on the plush white couch and talked about their lives. Aaron had plans to open a soul food restaurant on the south side of Chicago the following year. He asked Brooklyn about her writing projects and inquired about her relationship with Brian. She gave him detailed information about her upcoming book and quickly glossed over the conversation about her boyfriend. Aaron knew something was wrong.

"*Did he cheat on you again*?" he asked, already knowing the answer. Brooklyn shook her head, affirming his suspicion. She never concealed anything from Aaron because he could always see right through her. Aaron spent some time consoling his friend, but he wasn't able to hide his fury. He reminded Brooklyn about the numerous times her boyfriend had done similar things in the past. Brooklyn listened, but she didn't need to be reminded of the pain Brian had caused. Her mind was already made up. Their relationship was over. She would end it as soon as Brian returned to Atlanta.

Brooklyn and Aaron spent the rest of the afternoon together, they participated in workshops, had dinner and attended the late night party hosted by celebrity actor Shemar Moore and model Tyra Banks. She was pleased to spend time with her friend. Aaron was a much needed distraction from her troubles.

The early morning community service project was a huge success. The group of Blogalicious attendees was able to repaint a homeless shelter that hadn't received repairs in a number of years. They donated blankets, pillows and toiletries along with other needed items. Brooklyn noticed a woman sitting in the corner of the shelter's cafeteria. She was downcast, and slumped in a chair. Brooklyn adjusted her exercise pants around her waist and walked over to the woman. She raised her head and smiled, exposing her missing teeth. The woman began to tell Brooklyn about her daughter. The girl had run away with her boyfriend years ago and hadn't been seen or heard of since . The woman was incredibly sad, but expressed thanks that Brooklyn came to sit with her. Brooklyn hugged her and left the table. But not before giving the woman a twenty dollar bill that she had stuffed inside her shoe before leaving the hotel.

The afternoon flew by. Brooklyn attended three workshops and held another book signing. By the time the charter bus arrived at the hotel to take conference attendees to the Las Vegas strip, she was exhausted. She boarded the bus with her fellow bloggers and headed towards the Venetian Resort. Their guides met them at the back entrance of the massive hotel. Brooklyn was anxious to get out of the underground parking area because the fumes from the charter bus left her nauseous. The bloggers were escorted through the shopping area of the hotel. Brooklyn marveled at the bright signs that lined the resort. She had an urge to enter Tiffany's to pick up a piece of jewelry to commemorate her trip, but Selena urged her against it, noting the cost of such an item. Both ladies stopped in front of Neiman Marcus and swooned at the shoes on display in the store window. As the group entered Tao Nightclub, they were all carded and handed a small cream colored satin bag. Brooklyn rested on a brown leather couch in the seating area of the club beside her group members and opened the bag. She pulled out a pair of satin bedroom slippers with a note. "*You may be able to party all night, but your feet can't hang. Pull off those high heels and keep the party going. Love, The Venetian*" Brooklyn stuffed the slippers back in the bag and felt a jolt as Aaron pulled her from the couch. He lead her to the dance floor and began to move to the music. She was resistant because the smell of cigarette smoke made her feel sick, but she enjoyed the attention. He wrapped his arms around her waist and rubbed her back while they danced. She was amused. "*Are you drunk already*?" she laughed in his ear. Aaron's only response was to pull her closer to him. He breathed heavily on her neck and continued to dance.

Brooklyn reminisced about her friendship with Aaron. Over the years the two had shared many intimate moments. They were college sweetheart but Brooklyn's career goals stood in the way of their relationship. Aaron wanted to marry her, but she was determined to earn her Ph.D in English literature and become a professor at an accredited university. After Brooklyn turned down his marriage proposal Aaron moved to Chicago and began working as head chef for the Chicago Bears organization before landing a job with the mayor. Brooklyn moved to Atlanta to complete her graduate program at Emory University. The two found common ground through blogging. They remained friends and saw each other at various blogging conferences.

Brooklyn allowed her cheek to touch the side of Aaron's face and she closed her eyes. He slowly moved his hands down her back. The lower his hands moved, the tighter she held him. Aaron's lips grazed Brooklyn's cheek and she turned her face to his. He kissed her, slowly pressing his lips to hers. A soft moan came from Brooklyn while she rubbed the back of his neck.

As the charter bus backed out of the underground parking lot, Aaron and Brooklyn sat beside one another with their hands touching on the arm rest of adjoining seats. Brooklyn closed her eyes and rested her head on Aaron's shoulder. He smelled like a mixture of cologne and cigarette smoke. She awoke to his voice whispering in her ear. "We're here." Wiping her eyes, Brooklyn arose from her seat and exited the bus. Her mind spun with thoughts of their kiss. She wanted to ask him to spend the night with her. Instead, she told him goodnight, then headed to her suite alone.

Chapter 2

BRIAN MATTHEWS WATCHED in amusement as the heavy set women grabbed the bottoms of their colored skirts and sang in unison "*Welcome to Jamaica*!" The women stood at the entryway of gate 11 in the Ian Fleming International Airport. Brian walked along the corridor smiling at each of them. He thought them to be beautiful. Much to large for his taste, but beautiful none the less. He and his travel mates boarded a white van that waited in the parking lot of the airport. The van jolted as it rounded a curb at maximum speed. Brian braced himself when he spotted a cow in the middle of the dirt road. The driver did not slow his pace to allow the animal to pass, yet sped up and honked his horn to hurry the bovine along.

The dirt roads of Ocho Rios were covered in puddles from the heavy rain of the previous night. Brian eyed the lavish hotels lining the unpaved streets. A stark contrast from the broken down shacks and impoverished looking pedestrians along the opposite side of the muddy road. The driver stopped abruptly and hopped out of the vehicle. He quickly began removing his passengers' luggage from the trunk. Brian exited the van and stretched, gazing at the sky. The Jamaican sun sat on a bed of clouds, turning the sky a bright orange. He adjusted his baseball cap and squinted his eyes as he looked toward the water. Even with the setting sun the ocean remained a clear, bright blue. A dreadlocked, scraggly beard native approached Brian. "*Greeeeetin, sah,*" The Jamaican said with a smile. "*You smoke?*"

The Jamaican shoved a marijuana blunt in Brian's face. Brian watched the trail of smoke rise into the air. He took the blunt into his mouth and inhaled.

"*Ganja. Niiiiiiiice! Dere's more where dat came from... for de right price, of course.*" His tar stained teeth shone through his lips as he smiled in anticipation. Brian reached in his pocket and passed the Jamaican a twenty dollar bill. In turn the Jamaican stuffed two tightly wrapped blunts in Brian's hand, mumbled some patois and sauntered away. Brian refocused his gaze back on the crystal blue water in the distance as he thought about home. He had only been in Jamaica for a few hours but was already homesick. He thought to call Brooklyn the moment he arrived to his hotel room but the sight of the Jamaican hotel attendant prolonged his call. She was tall and dark. The curve of her hips made Brian lift his brow. He was spellbound by the flow of her hair and the arch of her cheekbones. The woman, with no regard to Brian's gaze, handed he and his company their individual room keys and bid them farewell as she answered a ringing phone.

The next day proved to be a busy one. The volunteers assembled at Trelawny Independent Day School and worked until sundown laying brick and mortar. There were electricians, plumbers, painters and construction crews all navigating around one another in an effort to quickly rebuild what had been lost. Brian took a break from his labor to video their progress. He interviewed the volunteers, school leaders and students. They all applauded Brian and his cohorts for their work in bringing the needed supplies and manpower. He would spend time that night editing the footage and uploading it to his school's YouTube channel. This video would prove to be a great marketing tool for Atlanta Leadership Academy for Boys. Community service was one aspect of the school's charter that needed to be fulfilled in order to remain open.

Brian's legs were covered in mud. There was a thick film of wet earth that surrounded his boots. The air smelled of metal and wood. From each corner of the rebuilt structure came a heavy noise of material being thrown about, nails being hammered, and wood being ground. The volunteers were ahead of schedule and the excitement in the air caused everyone to work with careful speed. The students' desks, science lab equipment and library furniture would all be delivered that week. Carpenters knelt on floors in the finished wing of the building installing carpeting. Lena Drummond, the schools headmistress, sat in her car finalizing the delivery schedule for the cafeteria tables and kitchen appliances. Brian walked by her car just as she ended the call. Lena tapped on her window and motioned for Brian to come closer. Through the glass he watched a burst of fog explode from Lena's mouth onto the window pane as she shouted in her Jamaican accent "*Come, man! Sit wit me here*!" He obliged and walked towards the car.

Lena was dressed in a purple T-shirt and Levi jeans. Her slender fingers gripped the steering wheel as Brian sat in the passenger seat. The two acquaintances talked briefly about the schools progress and the ribbon cutting ceremony that would be held in a few weeks. Lena thanked Brian repeatedly for the help he and the other volunteers gave. She also told him how appreciative she was of the thousands of dollars that Brian had collected and presented to the school administration to assist in the rebuilding efforts. They both watched as the work crews packed up their tools and closed the construction site for the night. It was late evening and the Jamaican sun had already begun to give way to the glowing moon. With the night approaching, Brian's body succumbed to exhaustion. He said his goodbyes to Lena Drummond and made his way back to the hotel.

Throughout the two weeks the volunteers worked tirelessly in rebuilding the school. By the end of Brian's trip all classrooms and offices were completed. The library, auditorium and playground were also finished. All that was left was the completion of the new gymnasium and the outdoor landscaping.

The travelers felt satisfied with their work and all boarded the airplane with a great sense of accomplishment. Brian settled into his seat feeling much lighter. When he got dressed that morning, before heading to the airport, he noticed how much bigger his pants appeared. He had to tighten his belt in order to keep them at his waist. During his ten days in Jamaica Brian had lost a substantial amount of weight. With the physical strain he endured and his heavy diet of fresh fruit, Brian was nearly fifteen pounds lighter.

At takeoff he reclined his head on his seat and tried to sleep. It was impossible to rest because his mind spun with the massive to-do list that awaited him. There were only nine days until the start of a new school year. As principal of Atlanta Leadership Academy for Boys, Brian was faced with new student registration, teacher orientation, a budget meeting with the school Board members and many other time consuming tasks. There was a rush of excitement in his spirit. Brian thought about the joy of seeing students walk the halls wearing their forest green shirts with the acronym *ALAB* emblazoned on their collars in gold letters. Brian was proud of his students. He made it a point to know each of them by name. He spent time going through each child's personal records. Once a student was admitted to ALAB Brian met with him and his parents at their home to welcome each child into the Academy's family. Throughout the school day, he could be seen walking the halls greetings his faculty and staff. It was common practice for the principal to mop floors when the custodians were overwhelmed, serve food when the cooks fell behind on the lunch schedule and sit in on classes when teachers needed a break. Brian was well respected by his staff and admired in the community for the job he had done at the school.

Brian expected to see Brooklyn as he exited the plane and made his way to baggage claim. But she was no where in sight. He checked his phone messages but had not received a call or text from her. After acquiring his luggage Brian walked to the car pick up lane. He stood for a moment anxiously awaiting his girlfriend's arrival. She should have been there by now. Perturbed, he called Brooklyn and became furious when she did not answer her phone. He hailed a cab and felt the beginnings of a headache as the cabbie drove him home.

Brian stood in shock as he entered his house. Initially, he didn't notice any difference but once he slung his luggage on the couch he noticed a few items missing from the living room. The bookshelf was nearly empty. Only a few sports books were left lying sideways on the shelf. He called out to Brooklyn as he walked down the hall. There was a hollow echo that met him as he entered the bedroom. The bed was stripped naked. The beautiful linen that Brooklyn had spent time picking out was not covering the bed as it was before his trip. Brian looked in the closet. The hundreds of shoe boxes that were usually lined along the walls had disappeared. Brooklyn's clothes weren't there either. Her designer purses were missing and her bathrobe that normally hung on a hook was gone as well. Brian rushed into the master bathroom. Her toothbrush, perfumes, makeup and hair accessories had vanished. He felt a chill come over him as he scoured the house looking for any semblance of Brooklyn. There was none.

Brian threw himself on the couch and thought. What could have gone wrong? He rubbed his temple and contemplated. He couldn't think of anything he had done or said to make Brooklyn move out. He called her again but there was no answer. Just as a small tear began to trickle down his face, Brian turned towards the fireplace to notice a sheet of paper hanging from the mantle. He sprung up and grabbed the paper.

"Brian, I'm glad you made it home safely. Congratulations on all you accomplished in Jamaica. I'm sure the students have a beautiful new building to enjoy. I've decided to move out. While you were gone I received a message from someone named Alisa Daniels. I'm sure you know who she is. Alisa told me some things about the two of you and I believe her. As you know, this isn't the first time this has happened. Please do not try to contact me. Our relationship is over. There's no need for us to discuss anything because my mind is made up. I wish you all the best. Brooklyn"

Brian's eyes grew as big as saucers with each word he read. Anger welled up in his soul. He crumpled the paper into a ball and with a tremendous growl, punched his living room wall, causing a lamp to shift. Brian laid back on the couch and massaged his temples, wondering what to do next.

He awoke late the next afternoon with a fierce pounding in his head. Brian rolled himself from the couch onto the floor and buried his head in the carpet, recounting the events of the night before. Throughout the night he had called Brooklyn's phone repeatedly. He left twelve messages before her inbox filled. Desiring consolation, Brian sought his brother's advice.

Community Cuts Barbershop was housed in a

shopping plaza adjacent to a bakery, dentist office, martial arts studio and Caribbean restaurant. Shoppers lined the sidewalks making their way to various stores. Patrons sat outside the barbershop on a wooden bench that was strategically placed for the overflow of customers. Under a neon sign hung a laminated sheet of paper with the words *free school supplies.* Notebooks, packs of paper, pencils, pens and art supplies lined a wall in the barbershop. A few customers scoured through the materials picking out 3 ring binders and crayons. Dexter Matthews, owner of the barbershop, looked up at his brother walking through the door. He wrinkled his brow at his disheveled sibling and rose from his chair to greet Brian. Dexter watched his brother wave at the company of men and make his way to the back of the barbershop.

Dexter followed his brother. Then tentatively closed the door to his office and sat. Sitting in a slump, staring at the floor, Brian told Dexter the sordid details of the previous night . He confessed his relationship with Alisa Daniels, expressing complete sorrow for his lapse of judgment. With his voice quivering, Brian began to wonder aloud where Brooklyn could be living - what she was doing. Dexter lost patience with Brian's sulking. He called his brother an imbecile and rolled his eyes. This wasn't the first time he lodged insults at his brother. After each of

Brian's affairs he had called him such names. *Idiotic tramp, loser, disgusting ass,* and *fool,* were all names that had been thrown in Brian's direction. Dexter was clueless as to the reason Brian would mistreat Brooklyn in such a way. Throughout the afternoon Dexter tended to his customers, keeping his eye on the office door. He didn't have many words of consolation for his brother. But he did worry about his condition. Brian had confined himself to the barbershop office for hours.

Inside the office, Brian typed furiously with his thumbs. This would be the 5th text message sent to Brooklyn that day. Each time he pressed send Brian waited with anticipation for a response. There was none. He was at a complete loss. He called all of Brooklyn's friends. He dialed her office number repeatedly and left several messages. He thought vigorously about where she could be but had no idea where to start looking. Feeling overwhelmed with worry and shame Brian unlocked the office door and slowly exited the room. He stuffed his hands in his pockets and looked around. Dexter was arguing with Marcus, co-owner of the barbershop, about the Atlanta Falcon's preseason game that aired the night before. The Falcons won, in overtime, on a three point conversion play that Marcus thought was a holding penalty against the Falcons. But Dexter, being a staunch fan would not let him get a word in edgewise against his beloved team.

The conversation ceased when they noticed Brian standing at the back of the shop.
With all eyes on him, Brian stuck his chin in his chest and sauntered towards the front door. Marcus, feeling amused, asked Brian how he was feeling. Brian did not answer, yet stuffed his hands deeper in his pockets and walked out the door.

Chapter 3

DRIPS OF SWEAT TRICKLED DOWN Brooklyn's face. She grimaced in pain as she attempted to complete the last of twenty burpees. As she rose from the floor her trainer gave her a high five and walked over to a tricep machine to adjust the weight. Brooklyn followed. Emory pointed at the seat, commanding Brooklyn to sit down. "*This was supposed to be an easy day,*" Brooklyn said with a note of irritation. "*If you want easy, you need to train yourself.*" Emory snapped back.

The pair had trained together for nearly a year. After her car accident, Brooklyn decided she needed something to take her mind off of her miscarriage. So she began to work out at a furious pace. Exercise had become Brooklyn's refuge. She used it to clear her head when work became too demanding or Brian became too complacent. It was easy for Brooklyn to release her frustrations with an hour on the elliptical machine, yoga class, or intense weight lifting. Emory made sure that Brooklyn utilized her time wisely in the gym. Not a moment was wasted when they trained together. Emory helped Brooklyn shed 17 lbs from her frame and gain a more chiseled, healthy look.

After each of their sessions Emory would jot down Brooklyn's work out schedule for the upcoming week. Brooklyn made sure she followed her trainer's instructions to the letter. She was happy with the results she'd achieved and continued making exercise a priority, even if she was in despair over her breakup with Brian.

Brooklyn threw on a t-shirt over her sweat-drenched body and said goodbye to Emory. On her way back to her new apartment she stopped by Jason's Deli to pick up a grilled chicken salad. Since moving to Atlantic Station, Jason's Deli had become her favorite eatery. She often stopped there to test out their menu items. It was a healthy alternative from the fast food Brian often opted for. With salad in hand, Brooklyn strolled through the lobby of her apartment building and smiled at the concierge. The *Twelve* apartment homes and hotel was positioned in the heart of Atlantic Station, a new "work, dine, play" development on Seventeenth Street in downtown Atlanta. This twelve-story structure consisted of two towers; one side - an apartment building, the other- a five-star hotel. The towers were connected by an upscale restaurant and bar that was a popular spot for Atlanta's elite.

Brooklyn's one bedroom loft apartment was exactly what she needed. It had only taken her a few days after returning from Las Vegas to find the space. She moved in swiftly, leaving thoughts of Brian behind. The remainder of that afternoon was spent updating her syllabi for the upcoming semester of classes. She only had a few days before the fall semester at Spelman College began. There was little time to upload each syllabus to her webpage for the registered students.

Over the past few weeks she had made every attempt to keep her mind occupied. She put up a barrier, blocking thoughts of Brian from her head space. Brooklyn didn't even bother listening to the repeated messages left on her phone. And she erased every email he sent without reading any of them. She gave her friends explicit instructions to not mention Brian for any reason. Brooklyn told them, in no uncertain terms, that her relationship with him was over. She had moved on with her life and had no desire to hear about him. They all respected her wishes. Brian made repeated calls to each of her friends but none of them told Brooklyn about his incessant questions. Brooklyn had not told any of her friends about the new apartment. She didn't want them to make the mistake of alerting Brian of her living arrangements. He wouldn't be able to find her. And that's the way she wanted it.

Once her syllabi were completed and uploaded to the school's website Brooklyn opened her manuscript and began to type:

Morally, Eugenia knew that killing another person was wrong. But any thought of Willie having an ounce humanity had long gone from her mind. He was a scoundrel, a rotten morsel of a being that needed to be discarded from the Earth. She eyed the black butcher's knife that rested on her kitchen counter. It was a wedding gift from her sister, Willemina. As a teenager, Eugenia begged her mother to allow her to take a cooking class at Williamsburg Technological College. And since her mother, Doris, was a secretary in the administrative offices of the school, Eugenia could take the class for free. Eugenia loved cooking and often tested new recipes on her sister. Willemina could see how much Eugenia enjoyed cooking and often complimented Eugenia's dishes. Once Willie and Eugenia announced their engagement Willemina decided on the perfect wedding gift for her sister.

Willemina was a nanny for a white family. Braxton Lawry and his wife, Helen, had the most God-awful children. She thought about quitting her job every single day. But she wanted to buy her sister an expensive knife from BC Moore's department store, so she stayed on as a nanny and managed to save the $37.00 needed for purchase. With pride, Willemina strolled into BC Moore's and pointed at the chef's cutlery set that sat behind the counter. The saleswoman picked up *the knives and placed them on the counter. "You have enough money to buy this, girl?" "Yes, ma'am." Willemina slowly poured the money into the saleswoman's pale white hand and smiled.*

Eugenia missed her sister. And as much as she hated Willie, she decided that she wouldn't dare defile her sister's memory by spilling Willie's drunken, evil blood on a knife that Willemina worked so hard to buy.

Eugenia walked onto her porch. She thought the fresh air would help her shake off the thoughts of murder. She rested her hands on her wide hips and looked up into the clouds. The cool breeze was a welcome change from the heat of yesterday. The brutal sun had hidden itself behind the clouds to allow the wind to blow. Eugenia stood for a moment, listening to the leaves rustle in the trees. A gray squirrel skipped along a branch and ducked into the trunk of the tree. Just as Eugenia swatted a mosquito that buzzed around her ear, Doctor Clyde Sable sauntered across the street into her yard. "Mornin' Ms. 'Genia. How you?" "Hey there, Clyde. You want something to eat? I got some lima beans and ham." "Yes, Ma'am. Put it in a tuppa ware bowl fa me en I'll eat it lata."

Eugenia did just as Doctor Clyde Sable asked and returned to the porch with his meal enclosed in a plastic Bi-Lo shopping bag. He thanked her kindly and continued on his journey down the street. Eugenia said a prayer to God that Doctor Clyde would not die from a heat stroke. She included in her prayer the desire for Doctor Clyde to find some proper summer attire. The black blazer and plaid scarf he wore were not fitting for the August heat. She thought he would soon faint.

Eugenia thought it odd that the man's given name was 'Doctor'. The story spread throughout the town was that his mother, Ms. Janie, was on the brink of death after the delivery of her son. The town doctor could not stop the bleeding. Ms. Janie, lying on the blood-soaked mattress began to pray profusely for her life to be spared so she might take care of her children. In the middle of her plea to God, she feel into a deep sleep. Ms. Janie's bleeding soon stopped and the doctor woke her with smelling salts. When Ms. Janie opened her eyes and saw her plump baby laying beside her she lifted her hands and praised God for her deliverance from death. She then looked over at the pale-faced doctor and say "thank ya, sir". To show her appreciation, she named her son in honor of the man who had helped bring him to life, and helped save hers. She called him "Doctor".

Thunder roared outside Brooklyn's window. The lightening flashed so brightly it made her jump. She shut down her computer, turned the lights off in her apartment then went to bed. She remembered her mother's words: "*When God is working we must be still.*" Brooklyn fell asleep with the sound of the rain beating against her window.

The next morning Brooklyn was awakened by the alarm on her phone. It was 7:00. She had three hours until her department meeting on campus.

Brooklyn mixed the waffle batter in a glass bowl and poured it into her hot waffle maker. She closed the lid and turned the waffle maker upside down to begin cooking. Taking a sip of her orange juice she picked up the remote and turned her TV to The Dan Patrick Show. Dan Patrick, the Emmy award winning sports broadcaster, was set to interview Ray Lewis, former Baltimore Ravens linebacker and two-time Superbowl champion. Brooklyn blushed as the camera focused on her favorite football player. She had long admired Ray Lewis since she interviewed him years ago for Brown Girl Magazine's *Most Eligible Bachelor* edition. Much to her surprise, Lewis showed poise and gentleness during their meeting, unlike his rugged, fierce demeanor on the football field. Lewis was so taken by Brooklyn's professionalism and knowledge of football, that he granted her several interviews throughout the years, all of which appeared on her popular YouTube channel. Once breakfast was done she readied herself for her morning meeting. Brooklyn was tired and in no mood to sit for hours listening to her department head talk. But this meeting was mandatory so she did her best to mentally prepare for the day.

Brooklyn had trouble staying focused through the meeting. Bryan's repeated calls and text messages were a distraction. She considered returning his call but quickly pushed that thought from her mind. She turned her phone off to avoid any more interruptions then turned her attention to the speaker.

Dr. Derek Washington wore a powder blue gingham shirt with a pair of black slacks. His silk blue tie was the perfect compliment to his attire. As he spoke, he smoothed the tie on his chest and smiled at the audience. He had been head of Morehouse College's English department for four years and worked diligently to ensure that the collaboration between Morehouse and Spelman was strong. Just as Dr. Washington turned to the Promethean board to display a table of the incoming freshmen verbal SAT scores a siren blared through the room. Brooklyn, accustomed to this type of interruption, closed her MacBook and gathered her materials. She followed her colleagues toward the exit and out the doors of the humanities building.

The midday heat gripped the campus. Brooklyn squinted her eyes and searched for a tree that would give some relief from the sun. She watched as the fire engine rushed through the campus, coming to a halt in front of her coworkers. For the past two weeks the fire alarm in the humanities building would sound for no apparent reason. It was believed to be faulty wiring. The electrical engineers had attempted to correct the problem numerous times. But each visit only caused another false alarm.

Brooklyn shifted her weight from one leg to the

other as Dr. Washington approached her from behind. "*I brought something for you,*" he said in a sultry voice. Brooklyn lifted an eyebrow and bit her bottom lip to conceal her smile. She turned towards the voice. His almond eyes shone bright. He gazed at her with a comforting grin. Dr. Washington lifted a book from his leather attaché case and handed it to Brooklyn.

It was an advanced copy of his upcoming novel, *Contemplating Death*. Months prior, Dr. Washington asked Brooklyn to read his manuscript and give her thoughts on the book. He respected her as a colleague and fellow author. They often discussed story lines, character traits and publishing. The professors enjoyed their collaboration and never missed their monthly meeting at the campus' Starbucks.

Brooklyn congratulated her friend on the book and assured him that she'd have it read by the end of the week. Against her better judgment, Brooklyn declined Dr. Washington's lunch invitation, then headed across campus towards the library.

The private study room was just what Brooklyn needed to ward off any distractions . She desperately needed time to write and planned to remain in the library until she had penned her rush of ideas. She stared at her computer screen blankly. Brooklyn placed her hands on her keyboard and waited. Her fingers did not move. She breathed slowly and listened to the silence that abounded. Motionless, she searched her mind for the characters that had been speaking to her all morning. They were gone. Brooklyn began to panic. Her breathing increased and beads of sweat appeared near her temples. Even in the stillness of the library Brooklyn was unfocused and anxious. Something was wrong. She thought of Brian and lifted her cell phone to call him. Shaking that thought from her mind, Brooklyn tossed her phone in her bag that laid on the floor. She pulled out the book that Dr. Washington asked her to read. Opening the book, she rested her head in the palm of her hands. She squinted her eyes at the opening lines and began...

Contemplating Death

"Farqua's Story"

Because of his tumultuous existence, Farqua decided to slit his wrist. He wrenched in pain as the blade slid across his arm. Without making a single sound he watched as the blood trickled from his body and gathered into a small pool on the bathroom floor.

His OCD made him want to immediately clean the mess. But it was futile. He would soon be dead. Lifting himself from the floor Farqua carelessly tossed the blade into the sink. It rattled, causing an echo to bounce from the walls. The distraught man breathed heavily and watched his chest rise and fall in the mirror.

Pulling a wet cloth from the counter he bent slowly and wiped the bright red blood from the tiles then tossed it in the sink along with the blade. He sat on the side of his tub.

Farqua waited for death to take hold but it never did. The cut was not deep and the blood had already stopped pouring. He felt lightheaded, hungry.

An episode of Sanford and Son played in the background. Walking past the TV he chuckled as Fred and Esther argued. Farqua pulled the refrigerator door open and felt the soreness in his wrist. He grabbed a container of grapes from the top shelf and sat in a slump at his kitchen table. He hugged the bowl. Farqua allowed his forehead to rest in the palm of his hand and with his damaged arm, lifted a grape to his mouth.

He resigned to the fact that he would live another day and contemplated a more effective way to kill himself. He would die tomorrow. Certainly, hanging himself would be quicker and less of a mess. Farqua's eyes looked in the direction of the ceiling. The wooden beams were worn, much too weak to hold his 165 pound frame. Besides, where would he get the rope?

Farqua's cell phone buzzed. He gathered his thoughts and raising his phone to his ear said a whispered, "Hello." He listened as the voice on the other end spoke in a brash tone. He closed his eyes and waited for the voice to cease. "Yes, yes. OK. Fine." Farqua ended the call and put another grape in his mouth.

A siren sounded. Farqua looked towards the window

and wondered what poor soul was being carted away in the ambulance. He walked across the room and peered towards the sunlight. There was a soft rainbow sweeping the sky. He was thankful the rain had stopped. He thought it cliché to kill yourself during a thunderstorm.

Outside his window a trumpeter sat on a bucket along the sidewalk. A black hat was turned upside down beside the musician's feet holding a collection of dollars and coins. Farqua watched as the trumpeter tapped his foot and lifted the instrument to his pierced lips. The music began. Farqua smiled.

Brooklyn lifted her head and wiped a tear from her eye. This will certainly be a depressing novel, she thought. She turned to the back of the book and stared at Dr. Washington's picture. A sense of sorrow came over her when she reminisced about his misfortune. This highly acclaimed novel, that had already sold thousands of pre-orders and won the author an interview with CNN did not come at a small price. A year before Derek Washington joined the staff of Morehouse College he worked as an associate professor at The University of North Carolina, Asheville. He and his wife, a violinist with the North Carolina Symphony took a long-awaited skiing trip to Greeneville, Tennessee. The long, winding road of Tennessee Highway 124 was unfamiliar territory to the couple. Dr. Washington gripped his steering wheel and squeezed his breaks as he maneuvered his SUV through the cliffs. A soft drizzle fell on their windshield as his wife began to sing *Great Is Your Mercy* to ease her nerves. She was terrified of heights. Just as they rounded a bend a deer jumped in front of the car. Dr. Washington's SUV swerved, skidding on an icy patch, and fell into a tavern on the side of a cliff. For three days Dr. Washington and his semi-conscious wife awaited rescue from the harsh Appalachian Mountains.

Dr. Washington used the sleeve of his sweater to stop the blood that gushed from his wife's head. As he cried and pleaded with God to save his love, she, in a daze, began to tell him things. Sensing her approaching demise she spent long hours sharing her heart with her husband. Contemplating her own death she spoke in soft tones. Each sentence began with "If I die...."

Dr. Washington's recovery was a hard fought battle. He suffered a fractured leg and ruptured spleen. He endured two surgeries to repair a broken clavicle. But his broken heart was his biggest hurdle of all. After learning of his wife's death the doctors had to deliver even worse news. His wife had been seven weeks pregnant with their child. Dr. Washington was crushed. He and his wife had tried unsuccessfully for years to conceive a baby. Thousands of dollars were spent on painful fertilization injections and procedures. They wanted nothing more than to be parents. They had almost given up hope when their fertility specialist encouraged them to be a part of a new clinical trial. This new medicine would increase his wife's estrogen, making her more fertile. Unbeknownst to the couple, it had worked.

Mourning the loss of his wife and unborn child, Dr. Washington joined a support group for grieving widows. These weekly meetings gave him some solace. He was encouraged by the many stories told by fellow attendees. Dr Washington began to write down these stories. He also began interviewing others who had suffered tragedies. He soon turned these interviews into fictional stories which became a 210 page novel. "*Contemplating Death*" won the author interviews with CNN, C-Span, and the Melissa Harris-Perry Show. He also appeared on PBS radio and in various magazines.

Brooklyn was excited about her friend's success. And happy that he had found a road to recovery and healing. She spent the remainder of the afternoon in the private study room of the library reading the first few chapters of *Contemplating Death.* She lifted her head only for a brief moment when she heard voices outside the study room. Brooklyn watched as two students passed the window carrying a stack of books. She sighed heavily as she rubbed her temples then rested her forehead on her fist. Brooklyn turned her attention back to her book and focused her eyes on the next chapter.

"Lani and The Baby"

Lani remembers arriving at the abortion clinic with her stomach in knots. It was a Saturday morning. Early. The clinic wasn't opened yet. Lani thought how surprisingly peaceful the parking lot appeared. Where were the angry protestors with their picket signs displaying pictures of dead, bloody fetuses?

Lenny haphazardly drove the car near the entrance of the clinic, stopped abruptly and forcefully put the gear in park. He was angry. Lani watched him rub his eyes and scratch his unkempt beard with his middle finger. He glanced at her.

She reluctantly lifted her eyes and watched his nonverbal pleas to go back home. Lani knew how badly her boyfriend wanted to keep the baby but her mind was made up.

They had argued furiously the week before. "Why are you doing this?" he asked in earnest. After half an hour of spouting the many reasons she would not have a baby, Lenny sank into a leather chair, admitting defeat. "I can't believe you are going through with this" were his final words.

For the previous five days they communicated only through text messages. She told him what time the procedure was schedule and when he needed to pick her up. He responded "OK" and showed up on time to drive her to the clinic.

A shade was lifted from inside of the glass door of the clinic. A pale-faced woman wearing scrubs stared out of the door while sipping from a coffee mug.

Without hesitation, Lani sprung from the car and forged her way towards the woman on the other side of the door. "Good morning!" she said as she blew into her coffee mug. "Hi," Lani responded shyly. She followed the woman to the reception desk and looked around in trepidation.

The brash knock on the study room door caused Brooklyn to jump in fright. She looked up to find a library assistant tapping his watch through the glass window. The library would close in half an hour. Irritated by the nagging pain in her forehead, Brooklyn gathered her things and headed across campus to her car. She walked swiftly, but felt secure with the lighted walkways and numerous checkpoints throughout the campus. Once in her car Brooklyn checked her messages. She raised her eyebrow in shock as she listened to the voice on the other end of the phone. It was a message from her sister, Bailey.

Chapter 4

Marley and Tatum rounded the coffee table and stood with their hands resting on its side. The twins faced one another and giggled as they began to count: "*One, two, three....one, two, three...one, two, three... one.*" Brooklyn watched her nieces practiced their plies with precision. She quickly corrected Tatum's turnout and smiled as the girls continued. Their red and black tutus were wrapped in plastic hanging on a doorknob in Brooklyn's apartment. That night, the girls would give their debut performance at the Little Ballerina Dance Academy's end of summer showcase. Their 5-year old bodies couldn't contain the excitement as they pranced around their aunt's living room with glee.

Brooklyn didn't show much emotion when she checked her phone and noticed a missed call from Bryan. She helped the twins tie their shoelaces and headed downstairs. The girls squeezed their aunt's hands tightly and strolled down the sidewalk at

Atlantic Station. Brooklyn could barely keep up with their incessant chatter. They pointed at cars, laughed at mannequin in store windows and carefully walked on the tips of their toes. Brooklyn feigned attentiveness and nodded her head slowly as the girls asked questions about the new toy store that opened in the neighborhood. They were overjoyed that their aunt would purchase ballerina dolls for them.

Brooklyn felt her phone vibrate on her hip. *"Your phone, Aunty! Your phone!"* Marley held her new doll in one hand and tried to grab the vibrating phone with the other. Brooklyn quickly removed the phone from its holster and answered the call. As the trio walked towards the ice cream shop Brooklyn listened as her sister ranted about a pair of nude tights the twins needed for their recital. This was an identical performance from the night before. Bailey called Brooklyn in a panic. Brooklyn listened as her sister whined about the alternator on her Mercedes that had gone bad. She was stuck on the side of I-20 and needed Brooklyn to get the girls from dance rehearsal and keep them overnight while she got the car fixed. Exhausted with the conversation, Brooklyn turned her attention to a white Range Rover that slowly crept along the street. She watched as the tinted window rolled down. She squinted her eyes to focus on the smiling face from inside the vehicle. It was Dexter. Pleasantly surprised, Brooklyn returned the smile and waved vigorously. The twins watched as he parked his car and greeted Brooklyn with a hug.

Brooklyn, the twins and Dexter all sat outside Kilwin's Chocolate Shop enjoying the sun. Chocolate ice cream dripped down Tatum's chin. She quickly licked her face in an attempt to catch every drop with her tongue. Marley pointed at a clown who walked along the sidewalk juggling red balls in the air.

Dexter's effortless conversation was comforting. Brooklyn did not have to hide her disappointment with Dexter's brother. But she continually assured him that she was adjusting to her life's changes. After nearly an hour of talking, the group said their good-byes and Brooklyn headed back to her apartment to prepare the girls for their dance recital.

Autumn arrived sooner than Brooklyn had hoped. She wasn't quite ready for the cooler temperatures. The professor quickened her pace as she trekked across the campus of Spelman College. She didn't want to be late for her 10:00 am class. Brooklyn pulled the collar on her navy blue peacoat and stepped across a pile of leaves that accumulated in the front entrance of the Cosby Building. She waved to the leaf blower, giving him a warm smile. He nodded respectfully as he cleared the doorway of falling leaves and debris.

Brooklyn flipped the light switch in the classroom on the fourth floor of the English department. She heard the rumbling of students in the hallway making their way to class. The professor stood at the podium and powered on the computer and projector that sat in the front of the room. For the next fifty minutes she would listen to students give presentations on there analyses of the ways in which social protest has changed with the advent of social media sites like Twitter and Instagram. The professor stood at the end of class and, with a monotone voice, explained to her students that they all would need to make improvements and resubmit their assignments at their next class meeting. Ignoring the defeated moans that came from the crowd of academics, she picked up her blue peacoat and walked out the door disappointed.

In her office, Brooklyn sat staring at a photograph of Muhammad Ali. She eyed the beads of sweat that had accumulated on his forehead as he rested ringside with his elbows on his knees. On an adjacent wall there was a poster from The Toni Morrison Society's Fifth Biennial Conference held in Charleston, South Carolina. Beside that was a photograph of she and her favorite writer, Nikki Giovanni. The photograph was blown up to three times it's original size. It was displayed in a wood carved frame that was handcrafted at a flee market in Decatur, Ga. As an undergraduate student at Clemson University, Brooklyn had an opportunity to attend a seminar featuring the poet. Dr. Howard Keeling, head of the African American Studies Department at Clemson had arranged for his brightest pupils to be a part of the audience. As the crowd applauded the conclusion of the poet's talk Brooklyn rushed to the microphone that was set up in the aisle. With tears in her eyes and a pounding heartbeat she looked up at Nikki Giovanni and said, *"It's not often that a person gets to meet their hero. But today, I've met mine. Thank you for everything you've written. You are my inspiration."*

Brooklyn blew gently into her coffee mug and took a sip. The hot liquid burned her mouth. She pressed her lips together to numb the pain. As she opened her email inbox, Brooklyn eyed seven new messages, all from Brian. She considered opening each of them but quickly pushed that thought from her mind. With a swift click of her mouse the professor deleted the unopened messages.

Throughout the afternoon Brooklyn entertained a host of students seeking advisement on their pending research papers and presentations for her classes. She was able to ward off an encroaching headache by taking aspirin before her evening appointment with Dr. Washington.

Derek Washington was dressed in brown slacks and a silk bowtie. The crisp white shirt accented his biceps and Brooklyn couldn't help but notice the strong slope of his shoulders. He greeted her with an eager smile and opened his arms, inviting a hug. The smell of his cologne was mesmerizing. As she fell into his embrace Brooklyn's heart pounded. He eased his hand down the small of her back and let he hair tickle his nose. He allowed his cheek to brush against her skin. He held her close and realized, for the first time, that he loved her. For the remainder of the night he fumbled through their conversation in an effort to conceal his new-found feelings.

The joy Brooklyn felt after her meeting with Dr. Washington was short lived. She stood at the front door of her apartment in shock. The hallway was quiet except for the faint buzz of the elevator climbing to a higher floor. Brooklyn stared at the neatly written letter attached to her door.

If you only knew the pain
I feel each day when I open my eyes
or the way my heart breaks at the thought of you
tears fall each time I hear your name
I am losing sleep
My mind is scattered, shattered in pieces
Only your touch can make me whole again
If I could simply hear your voice
I cry out to you but my echo is the only answer
My God! How I need you in my life to wipe away
the pain- this gut wrenching desire I have for you.
I cannot breathe

I cannot breathe

The ominous note was from Brian. How had he found her? No one outside of her sister and nieces knew where she had moved. Brooklyn was careful not to alert anyone of her current living arrangements. Even when Dexter saw her walking with the twins to Kilwin's Chocolate Shop she made sure he was long gone before heading into her building. But now, somehow, Brian knew. He had been there.

Brooklyn felt a slight chill rush down her spine. Anger consumed her at that very moment. She was furious that her privacy had been compromised. She had put her tumultuous relationship with him behind her. And she hoped that he'd do the same.

Timidly, she put her key in the keyhole and unlocked the door. Brooklyn's heartbeat raced as she stood at her entrance listening to the silence. The possibility of Brian being an unwelcome guest in her apartment was too much to bear. Flipping the light switch, Brooklyn scanned her apartment for the intruder. She was alone.

Unable to sleep, she read Brian's note a million times in an attempt to decode its meaning. Just as the sun began to rise Brooklyn fell into a quiet sleep, with the note laying on her chest.

It was a rare occurrence for the professor to

cancel her classes. But she felt ill. The thought of Brian being at her apartment gripped her with a mixture of fury and fear. That day she stayed in bed updating her blog and approving numerous comments left by her readers. At noon she received a call From Dr. Garrett, a professor in the English department at Spelman College. With a muffled voice Professor Garrett alerted Brooklyn that she had had a disturbing visitor at her office. She listened as her coworker told her of a disheveled man with an unkempt beard and wrinkled clothing who belligerently asked for Brooklyn's whereabouts. Professor Garrett threatened to call the police, causing the man to leave.

For the next few weeks Brooklyn lived with a heightened awareness of her surroundings. She was careful to always get home before dark and tried to avoid walking alone. Brooklyn had heard that Brian got into a fist fight with his neighbor. The police weren't called but he had suffered a broken finger. News of Brian's aggressiveness was overwhelming. These repeated disturbances wouldn't fair well for his public persona nor his career. Her mind was swirling with thoughts. She was worried, anxious, consumed with a blend of anger and concern. Brooklyn dared not call him so to ease her mind she opened her laptop and began to write:

The music from the upright piano reverberated through the hot Sunday afternoon air. Son Montgomery sat on a rick-

ety stool rocking back and forth to the music, causing his seat to shake. The blue fabric on the stool had long ago turned a pale brown. The stool seemed to slowly whither away under the weight of the old man as he pat his foot. Son Montgomery struck the piano keys mercilessly causing the melody to bounce around the makeshift church. In between chords he looked out into the empty pews. He watched as a mouse crept across the floor in search of any left-behind food particles. He thought for a moment to lift his hands from the piano keys and throw an empty Coca Cola bottle at the rodent. But he did not want to anger his mother.

Mother Marie sat in the adjacent kitchen shelling peas. Her enlarged knuckles were sore from arthritis but that did not deter her from preparing Sunday dinner. She had a dirty scarf tied tightly around her head to protect the plaits that shaped her scalp. The woman hummed softly to the tune that her son played on the piano. For hours, he played as Mother Marie moved through the kitchen jostling with pots and pans.

"May not come when you wanna
But he'll be there right on time.
He's an on-time God,
Yes! He is!"

Despite his missing teeth, Son Montgomery sang loudly. He wanted to make his mother proud. "We sing about Jesus to keep the devil away!" Is what she always said. So, he increased the volume in his voice to make sure that the devil would stay miles and miles away from him and his momma.

Son Montgomery looked out at the horizon. As the sun began to descend he pulled the piano lid down on the keys and rose from his seat. The crook in his back caused him to walk hunched over, looking like a Neanderthal. He shuffled his feet across the wooden floor, grabbing the walls to support his weight. Son Montgomery followed the aroma of fried chicken, cabbage, peas and white rice. Sitting at the kitchen table the old man stared at the ready-made plate before him. With his eyes closed tight he began a fervent prayer:
"Oh God, my God,
Oh! how you have blessed us!
Lord, we thank ya for the Cross.
We thank ya for sending your
Precious son, Jesus, who gave his life for us.
Lord, we are wretched.
Lord, we are unworthy.
Lord, we are sinners.
But because of the precious blood
that was shed on Calvary's Cross
We are made new…."

Son Montgomery's voice filled the room. It spilled out of the windows and fell into the street, flowing to his neighbor's yards. Eugenia rocked in a wooden chair on her porch and listened to the prayer. Oddly enough, she found comfort in his words. Son Montgomery continued:
"…so Lord, I lift up my
hand to ya now. I

praise your name right now.
I worship ya right now, Lord.
We love you, God."

Droplets of sweat formed in the wrinkles of Son Montgomery's forehead. His breathing was labored and tears streamed down his face. His voice cracked with each word. The old man swayed back and forth with fervor as he talked to God:
"...Now, God, in the mighty name of
Jesus the Christ, ruler of all things,
we ask that you touch this food that it may
bless and strengthen our bodies.
Now to him who is able to do exceedingly
abundantly above all we could ever ask
Or think, we say Hallelujah! Praise God!
Amen!"

Mother Marie opened her eyes and gave her son a nod of approval. The woman gathered a heap of rice onto her fork and lifted it to her mouth. The pair ate the remainder of their Sunday dinner in silence.

Chapter 5

The Bethlehem Baptist Church choir filed onto the pulpit and made their way towards the choir stand. Their bright red robes kissed the floor as they walked. Poinsettias were aligned in a row concealing the massive speakers that sat on stage. Brian adjusted his silk tie and shifted slightly in his seat. He scanned the church repeatedly throughout the service but there was no sign of Brooklyn. It had been six months since she attended Bethlehem and Brian's fury was increasing with each unsuccessful search for his love.

The upcoming Christmas vacation would be a welcomed break. The stress of Brian's personal life was becoming too much to bear. He was unable to focus on work and the students and staff had noticed changes in his demeanor. He told himself how stupid it was to cause such a scene at Brooklyn's job. He vowed to stop drinking and try to be rational about the situation. "*Brooklyn will forgive me,*" he thought to himself as the choir began to sing. "*There's no way she can stay angry forever. If she doesn't forgive me I'll....*" He shook the evil thoughts from his mind and tried to focus on the music. Choir members swayed back and forth as the pianist pounded his fingers on the keyboard. Brian eyed the baptismal pool and watched the water vibrate to the beat of the drum.

Shuffling his feet back and fourth Brian adjusted his shirt collar. He wiped the sweat from his brow and brushed a piece of lint from his pants. The audience clapped their hands to the rhythm and sang in unison:

"I'm coming up, on the rough side
of the mountain. I must hold to God,
his powerful hand.
I'm doin' my best
to make it in!"

Angry that Brooklyn decided against attending church that Sunday, Brian got up from his seat and tipped out of the sanctuary. Weaving through rows of cars Brian felt the cool December air beat on his face. He stuffed his hands inside the pockets of his coat and sunk his chin deep into his chest. He sped down the interstate towards Brooklyn's apartment with blind fury. Brian dialed Brooklyn's phone repeatedly but there was no answer. He pounded his fists against the steering wheel and pressed harder on the gas pedal.

The blue lights that flashed in Brian's rear view mirror startled him. He had no time to trifle with police. He needed to find Brooklyn. Gripping the steering wheel tighter Brian considered the possibility of a high speed chase. But he knew the outcome would be disastrous. He decided to slow his speed and pull over. With the $189 speeding ticket in hand Brian suspended his search for Brooklyn and returned home distraught.

Early the next morning the sunrise poured into Brian's window, creating a glow on his sleeping face. Brooklyn's birthday usually brought joy to his heart but on this day he was lying in a bed of depression surrounded by a pool of grief and despair. He arose. And with no thought of washing his face, slipped his feet into a pair of sneakers that were thrown haphazardly across the floor. The Atlanta traffic was lighter than usual. With the holiday break there were no school busses littering the highway. He pulled into an underground parking garage and made his way up the elevator. Brian avoided making eye contact with anyone. His mind was cluttered with thoughts of Brooklyn. "*It's her birthday*," he said in a muttered tone. "*We have to celebrate.*" He shuffled back and forth on the elevator. Brian wiped the sweat from his hands and walked off the elevator, pushing past a young resident. He rounded the corner and gazed at Brooklyn's door. He stroked his hands across the gold painted apartment number and knocked softly. Slowly placing his ear against the door he listened for any movement inside. He heard nothing. Brian knocked again and was startled when a dog began barking down the hall. He pulled a crumpled paper from his pocket and shoved it underneath the door frame. Angry, Brian punched the door and stormed back to his car.

Brooklyn stood over her mother's tombstone and watched the grass sway slowly in the cold December wind. It had been three years since she observed the grave diggers lower the body into the ground. Now, brightly colored green grass replaced the overturned dirt that had been thrown over the silver casket those years before. Derek Washington stood in the distance watching his friend mourn her dead mother. He allowed her privacy during this solemn moment. During their hour-long drive to Braselton, Georgia he listened as Brooklyn gave a detailed account of her mother's untimely death.

Derek had invited Brooklyn to a weekend retreat at Chateau Elan Winery and Resort as a birthday present. She eagerly accepted but asked if they could stop at Green lawn Cemetery on their way. That Sunday marked the three year anniversary of her mother's death and Brooklyn thought it time to finally visit the gravesite. Early that morning, instead of going to church, Brooklyn packed a bag and headed up I-85 with Derek.

They carried on an easy conversation-one that included politics, pop culture and literature. It wasn't until they had almost reached their destination that Brooklyn began speaking of her mother. As she talked Derek grabbed her hand and listened.

"My mom was never sick a day in her life....never had a cold, never had the flu. I don't even remember her sneezing. She took vitamins, ate healthy, exercised regularly. She was in shape. She was happy. But one morning she took her puppy for a walk and collapsed on the sidewalk. She never got up. She was only 57."

The next day Brooklyn awoke to a bouquet of lilies seated on a stainless steel serving tray equipped with an omelet and glass of orange juice. "*Happy birthday,*" Derek greeted with a smile. Brooklyn admired the dimple that shown on his face. "*Thank you,*" she gushed. Brooklyn sat in silence enjoying her beautifully prepared breakfast as Derek returned to his room to get ready for the day. After a tour of the winery and a wine tasting that included exotic drinks like Port the couple spent the afternoon on the golf course.

Derek placed his hand on the small of Brooklyn's back and guided her through the hotel to their evening dinner reservation. Once seated at their table he began shuffling the glass salt and pepper shakers. The shakers spilled, leaving the white linen in a discombobulated state. "*Are you OK?*" Brooklyn asked carefully. Derek took a long, drawn out breath and pulled a small blue box from his pocket then placed it on the table atop the spilled condiments.

"*We've known each other for a long time. And I value our friendship. I know you've been going through a lot lately and I don't want to complicate matters. But I need you to know how much I care about you.*" Relieved that he was able to get the words out Derek took another breath and pushed the box closer to Brooklyn, encouraging her to open it.

Brooklyn fought back tears as she untied the carefully placed bow. She removed the box top to discover a sliver charm bracelet. She was delighted by the thoughtful gift. It was the exact bracelet she had pointed out to Derek on their numerous shopping excursions to Lenox Mall. Tiffany's was her favorite store. Brooklyn always found a way to drag Derek into the high-end jeweler for some window shopping.

She gingerly pulled the gift from its box and gazed at its beauty. She wiped a tear from the side of her face and thanked Derek repeatedly.

Throughout the night the pair discussed their future. The night ended with a concrete decision to travel to Myrtle Beach together during Spelman College's spring break. The couple kissed then departed to their own rooms.

The joy of Brooklyn's birthday celebration came to an abrupt end once she returned to her apartment. She stood in the doorway and clenched Brian's crumpled note in her hands with a mixture of fury and fear. *I will see you again. You can't hide.* The words burned Brooklyn's eyes as she repeatedly read the note. Brooklyn spent her evening at the Dekalb County Police Department filling out a police report and answering questions from the magistrate judge. The judge determined that there was, in fact, an imminent threat of harm due to the note being found inside her apartment. So, a temporary restraining order was issued. A court date was set for December 27th . That night Brooklyn headed to her sister house for insured safety. She couldn't risk having Brian show up at her apartment while she slept. Marley and Tatum had no mercy for their aunt's exhausted state. They wanted to stay up late making Christmas cookies and watching cartoons. Though distraught, Brooklyn obliged.

Eight days later Brooklyn stood before the judge and rubbed her temples in frustration and disbelief as the request for a permanent restraining order was denied. She looked across the courtroom at Brian. His suit was crisp and the yellow pocket square in his jacket added a bright touch to his gray pinstriped attire. When the hearing was adjourned Derek grabbed Brooklyn's hand and whisked her out of the courtroom away from Brian. She cried on her way home.

The start of a new semester at Spelman College was a welcomed distraction from Brooklyn's troubles. She sat in the dining hall sipping hot chocolate and eating a cinnamon roll. The professor watched as underclassmen unloaded boxes from their parent's cars and lugged them up the stairways to their dorm rooms. Before heading to her office she stopped at the campus bookstore to get matching Spelman t-shirts for her nieces.

"*Hey Dr. Knight*!" Brooklyn turned in the direction of the exuberant voice to see her former student standing behind the register with a stack of books in hand. Grace Turner's afro formed a beautiful halo around her head that made Brooklyn smile. She greeted her student then made her way to the second floor of the book store. She thumbed through the selections on the clearance rack and pulled two power blue t-shirts from the rail. "*The twins will like these*," Brooklyn said as she eyed the shirts. Her phone buzzed, interrupting her thoughts. She reached in her bag to answer the call but stopped in her tracks when she saw the number. It was Brian. She tossed her phone back in her bag with force and headed to the register to pay for the shirts.

The Spelman College English Department was

empty. Brooklyn saw the solitude as an opportunity to focus on her writing with no interruptions. She tossed her coat across the chair in her office and turned on her computer. She made the necessary updates to her syllabi and uploaded them to her school's webpage. She knew that the new crop of students were eagerly awaiting the class information. After writing a blog post and responding to numerous comments from her readers she dropped off the new t-shirts to her nieces and headed home.

A rush of cold air met Brooklyn at the door when she entered her apartment. She quickly turned on the heat to combat the winter temperature. Just as she walked into her bedroom she heard a shuffling behind her. She quickly turned. There was Brian leaning against a wall in the corner of her living room. Brooklyn was frozen with terror.

"*How did you get in here*?" Her voice quivered as she asked the question. Brian said nothing but peeled his body from the wall and slowly moved toward her. Noticing the gun that was wrapped in Brian's hand Brooklyn inhaled heavily and held her breath. She wanted to scream but could not make one sound. Her eyes widened as Brian hovered over her. He grabbed her by the neck and squeezed.

"*Didn't I tell you that you couldn't hide*?" Brooklyn could smell the alcohol emanating from his mouth. Brian threw her against a wall and watched as she collided with the floor. Pulling herself from the floor, she grabbed a glass vase that sat on her coffee table. She threw it toward Brian and watched as it shattered against the wall. Brooklyn ran towards the door then heard a resounding pop. She felt an unbearable sting in her back. Her legs gave way and she plowed into the floor.

Epilogue

THERE SHE WAS. The woman was sitting in a velvet green chair with bright eyes, a protruding belly, and round hips. Her golden brown legs stuck out from the bottom of her gown. Thick pink socks covered her feet which were enclosed inside a pair of brown slippers. The woman did not speak. She stared longingly at Brooklyn. Their eyes locked onto one another. The woman's face displayed a bit of sorrow, concern. "*I'm OK. I am OK.*" was the message her eyes conveyed. Brooklyn pleaded with the woman to speak. But the old lady said nothing. She simply sat in the corner of the room and stared at her beloved daughter.

Brooklyn remembered the green chair. Years ago, when Brooklyn was six years old, she sat in her first grade classroom at Willow Drive Elementary. Mrs. Lovely, her teacher, stood at the front of the room readying the chalkboard for the day's lesson. Brooklyn felt a tickle in her bladder. The six year old lifted herself from her desk and waited at the bathroom door for her friend, Tracey Wesley, to exit. The tickle in Brooklyn's bladder became stronger. She squeezed her eyes tightly and clenched her thighs to stave off the liquid from running down her legs. Finally, Tracey sauntered out of the bathroom singing her ABC's. Brooklyn rushed past Tracey and slammed the bathroom door. Just as she lifted her skirt, a stream of urine slid down her legs onto her new white lace socks. The embarrassed first grader walked hand in hand with her teacher to the school's office. Brooklyn waited patiently for her father to arrive. On their drive home she was told that a big surprise was awaiting her. Excited by the news Brooklyn rushed through the front door of their home only to find a small, seven pound baby sleeping on the velvet green chair. It was her sister, Bailey. Unbeknownst to Brooklyn, her mother had delivered the baby and was discharged from the hospital the following day.

For nearly thirty years that velvet green chair had symbolized life, joy and excitement. But as Brooklyn stood staring at her deceased mother the chair symbolized nothing but despair.

"It's not time. You can't join me just yet. You have to go back. Bailey needs you. Marley and Tatum need you. Take care of them."

Seconds later, her mother disappeared. Brooklyn stood staring at the empty green chair wishing the old woman would come back. She closed her eyes and began to feel excruciating pain flow through her body. She felt blood dripping from her back onto the carpet. Brooklyn tried to lift herself from the floor but was unable to move. A reverberation in the air froze Brooklyn with fear. She opened her eyes and saw Brian stumbling backwards. His uncontrolled body slammed into her glass bookshelf and he fell forward. His gun crashed against the carpet as his head met the floor. Brooklyn watched as blood spilled from a hole in his temple. Brian did not move.

Dressed in matching boots Marley and Tatum squealed with excitement as the snow began to fall. They both pressed their noses against the hospital window and watched the small white snowflakes make their way to the ground. Their mother whispered across the room for the girls to lower their voices as not to awake their sleeping aunt.

Bailey stared at her sister with concern. She watched as Brooklyn laid motionless in her hospital bed. Cords were protruding from under the sheets and machines beeped, monitoring Brooklyn's body functions. For the past few hours, Bailey's heart wrenched in pain at the uncertainty of her sister's condition. After receiving news of the incident she sat in the waiting room anticipating an update on Brooklyn's surgery. Derek hid the worry from his face as he tried to keep the twins entertained. His head spun with fear while sitting on the waiting room floor playing with the girls. He gazed at Bailey and winked his eye, insuring that all would be well. The doctor finally breezed through the door and headed towards the family.

"We removed the bullet from her back. She has lost a lot of blood but she will be fine. Your sister is in recovery right now. You can visit her for a few minutes. Then she'll be moved to her own room." Bailey remembered how her heart leapt when she heard those words from the doctor earlier that evening. The unspeakable joy she felt caused Bailey to lift her hands in praise and shout "hallelujah" through the waiting room. "*Jesus is real!! she screamed. "Thank you, Holy Ghost. Bless your wonderful Name!*"

Brooklyn's legs shuffled slightly. Bailey, Derek, and the twins rushed over to the bedside and gazed at the woman they all loved. She opened her eyes, looked at each of them and smiled.

ACKNOWLEDGEMENTS

To Stacey Ferguson and the Blogalicious Conference community, you have given my creativity a home and helped me become comfortable with my own imagination. Thank you for giving me a space to be free.

My deep gratitude to Dr. Michelle S. Hite of Spelman College for your vast intellect and Attorney Lashonda Council-Rogers for your expert legal advice. Thank you both.

To my husband – you are more than I could have ever prayed for. I thank God for thinking enough of me to put you in my life as my provider, comforter, confidant and friend. You are amazing. Thank you for believing that I can fly.

To my children – you have given me purpose. This book serves as proof that you must always push fear aside and follow your dreams. Mommy loves you. Thank you for giving me time to write.

CPSIA information can be obtained at www.ICGtesting.com
Printed in the USA
LVOW07s1150220415

435637LV00001B/6/P